Disclaimer:
I wrote this book almost four years ago, but I'd still love to share this story into the world.
There's no full plot. There's no logic. Especially when kids are running off into the forest alone, build a house (somehow haha) and tell their parents to get lost.
This story is mostly created just for fun. There's an end meaning. There's a story, but don't expect a giant titan to appear and for the main character to take I down.
It's mostly just a fun story I made, so I hope you'll enjoy it too!

Table of Contents

Prologue

I sat on the floor staring at the calendar in the room I shared with my sister, seeing if my family would even remember my birthday or even remember if I existed this time. Especially since they were often outside playing with Miss Perfect. Also known as, my twin sister, Rosemary. Rosemary was a few hours older than me and was born on January 6th, basically a day before me.

I heard the door close as Mom and Dad got into a fight as usual, shouting back and forth about which school Rosemary would be best at. None of it was about me. I was simple. My fate was already pre-decided by being born as a simple nobody without magic. I really didn't want to hear it today, since it was Christmas and I was turning four years old two weeks later. I never got a single present under the tree on Christmas, except for a simple 'You should be glad to be alive.' Meanwhile, Rosemary had a huge stack of presents under the tree.

I had a horrible start to the day, falling off the bed. The moment I woke up, my sister chose to prank me, of all things. She put soy sauce in the pancake syrup, so when I ate my pancakes, it tasted like a fistful of salt. When I came downstairs, I heard stuff about family and pictures and I had no idea what they were up to. I was only 3, so you can't blame me. My mind hadn't pieced it together quite yet. They were taking family pictures that day and as usual, I had no idea until I arrived to the scene. However, as always, by then, the picture was already taken and they had never noticed I wasn't in the photo. In any family photo.

My sister's blood contained pure magic. Both of my parents had half-magic blood running through their veins but I was unfortunate and didn't have a single drop of magic blood in my veins. In the world we live in, saying 'not having magic' isn't a very great thing, would be a huge understatement.

"Dawn! Come right here! Now!" Dad demanded in a strict tone.

There he was to call me to clean up after Rosemary who could barely read books or write or flush the toilet. Rosemary was a numbskull but really popular at her current school. I had to stay on an island that stood a billion miles away from the country where magic or half-bloods live on. All of us without magic, don't know how to swim or sail and we have to stay here our whole lives. If we are caught outside of this island, our heads would probably get chopped off. We are forbidden to learn how to sail or swim.

My hair was down today. I had dark brown to regular brown, wavy-straight hair. Three sections of my hair were actually black instead of brown. I had somewhat of a wolf cut, given the fact I'm not too sure what a wolf cut looks like.

I looked at the new picture on the wall, and a sharp wave of pain hit me here, in my heart. It was like I was invisible to my family. It hurt to look at the photo and I just wanted to smash it to the floor, 'til none of it was left. Suddenly, the window in my room shattered with a deafening crash, allowing a burglar to climb on inside. He smirked and took all of Rosemary's money and her treasures.

Despite disliking my sister, I couldn't help but shout, "Stop! You can't just take our stuff like that! I'm from a family of magic, you know?!"

The only thing I could think of was hitting the tough man covered with big muscles, with a metal baseball bat as hard as I could, not like I could expect much damage. He threw me a side easily and took everything good in the room and left.

I told Mom and Dad but as usual they completely ignored me.

It was nighttime now and I went over to Mom and Dad and I asked, "May I please sleep with you guys, I don't feel safe in my room with the whole burglar thing.

"No!" They both said in my face.

As I sauntered back to my room Rosemary asked the exact same thing I did, word for word. I sat in the corner of my room.

"Yes, of course darling!" They both agreed, "Then we will give you an extra safe room to sleep in and so you can stay away from the filth with no magic."

I was outraged why did Rosemary get to sleep with them and I couldn't. Every night, I'm shoved to the floor with all of Rosemary's kicking. My parents rearranged some stuff around and gave me a very old and creaky cot that had the smell of barf and unwashed piss. They didn't even fix the broken window. I lay awake all night in fear for my life, partially accepting my fate if I happened to die tonight. I ended up sitting in my closet alone all night, door locked and a barricade blocking anyone from entering.

Maybe if I ran away, they'd finally care about me for once. Just like how they care about Rosemary.

Chapter 1: A Sudden Big Move

"Hey!" my best friend Haven waved at me.

"Hey," I smiled weakly, as tired as humanly possible, "Another thievery in my room and I was basically sleeping in the closet all night again," I was too tired to speak in proper grammar at this point, so it was probably a random jumble of words, "The things in my closet has grown quite a lot. It would be quite a challenge to get in at this point. It is also quite a challenge to get out, so it sort of backfires. It's quite annoying if your sister is like basically world famous at this point."

I opened my backpack, which I made out of old rags and old clothes my sister was too big for. My sister was quite stupid. Idiotic. Gullible. But that's alright, because she's powerful and that's all that matters here.

"This is for you," I handed her the friendship bracelet that was safely stored in my 'backpack.'

"Thank you!" Haven smiled, admiring the bracelet.

Lydia came over, looking left and right, "My brother isn't here is he?"

"Nope!" I smiled, "Here, it's a friendship bracelet."

One by one, my friends came around, meeting us in our meeting place. Cai, was the only boy out of the five of us. His brown hair matched his caramel brown eyes, ears, and tail. He was an Alpha. Haven was also an Alpha but both Haven and Cai were Alphas with no magic. It's uncommon for an Alpha to not have magic but it still happens.

Lydia's cousin, Rose walked with us as usual. We were all great friends, "So what do you say about start babysitting and live on our own since well. We are all... invisible to our family. Or we are practically hunted down and in danger. If they go coo-coo on us because they actually care about us, I'm not going to flipping care. They didn't care about us when we needed them."

"Hmm... It's a good idea, but also not. I've thought about it for a long time but never saw it through, seen as how dangerous it potentially could be. But I'll go 'cause I'm not standing another night there. I could take Rosemary's bike. Still pretty new, but she doesn't like the colors so she's getting a new one," I shrugged.

Lydia thought, "But we are gunna need money to live."

"I'll take up babysitting," I said, "It's my 12th birthday anyway. Why does our school still have school days on holidays like Christmas? I mean, Christmas was two weeks ago, yeah, but why? We don't really get summer or winter breaks."

"I have absolutely no idea. Anyway, sure, you can do those jobs," Rose was getting excited to get away from her parent's cruel chores.

"But we can't leave yet because we don't even have enough money to rent a house yet," Cai whispered, "I'll also start babysitting and mowing lawns and shoveling snow since there is still a lot of snow. If there are leaves that is needed to be raked, I'll do that too."

"I'll do the same except babysitting since I am not old enough," Lydia and Haven announced in unison.

Rose and I both said, "We'll do the same as Cai, including babysitting."

"Alright!" Cai nodded. Excited, but he didn't show it, "Now let's get to our classrooms. See you at lunch!"

"See ya!" I left for class. We were all in different classes so we spilt up here and met up here at recess and lunch."

It was exciting. Not the best plan, running from adults in our lives, but I was truly fed up. Call me spoiled if you will, I had been invisible to my family for most of my life. I was also ignored all the time and I was always the laughing stock. I wanted to live in peace without my parents continuing to spoil Rosemary and seeing me as nothing.

I still wasn't in any family pictures and they had never noticed. Nothing changed about that. The only time they DID noticed me however, was when there was a chore everyone didn't want to do it and thought of me as their last resort. I could have a new chance at life, a new family. One could call us—me, a disgusting spoiled brat that doesn't honor what I've been given. Food, water, shelter, a life, but I don't care. You don't know what it's like until you've experienced it yourself. The pain we are stuck under since we were born...

Lydia and Haven helped us hang up flyers for our jobs. We didn't hang up any flyers for mowing lawns, however, since the grass was buried under inches of snow and putting that poster up would be something Rosemary would've done.

While hanging flyers up, I saw a sign that said, 'If you buy this land, then the entire forest and the road is ours. By it now, this year for a 75% off sale.' The original price was 100,000 dollars which meant the discount was 75,000 dollars. The forest was pretty small but worthy.

There was another sign on the right of the other one, the said, 'You make your house, we supply with all the wood, nails, paint, pipes, and etc. But you can hire people if you want, that's none of our business right there. Please. We are desperate to get rid of this land. We need the money.'

"Alright!" I said to myself just as the rest of us ran over to read the sign.

"Let's work for it, alright?!" Lydia shouted with glee.

"Yeah!" the rest of us said.

Cai joked, "We need the human calculator!"

They were referring to me since I was in a higher standard for both reading and math since the school thought I was good at reading and math. My friends either had a higher standard for reading or math and some didn't have a higher standard at all. We were each earning, 20 dollars an hour for babysitting and 20 dollars a driveway to shovel snow, and if needed, later, 20 dollars for raking one lawn, and 20 dollars a lawn to mow.

"We each need to do 750 jobs or hours of babysitting to get to our goal," I concluded, "We are going to have to keep track of our business thing. Could I be the treasurer?"

"Sure," Cai nodded.

"Yeah, as long as I get to take care of our activities and how long the babysitting jobs will be," Lydia nodded.

Rose thought, "I am good at advertising, so I could advertise."

Haven and Cai came up with ideas of what they would do to help as Haven said, "My little brother cared about me, as you know. My parents left this place to live on the magic island so I am now in an overcrowded sickening orphanage that hates me. At least he gave me his phone so I could call him. We could use that to get calls."

Cai continued to ponder our situation right here, "I don't know, I think I might want to be a backup for any of us in case one of us gets sick or hurt. I have a phone too."

We all stared at Cai with an expression that said, 'Where and when did you get a phone?'

"What?" Cai shrugged, "I took it, it was cracked and my family wanted a new one. I wanted to give it another chance to well... live. It can still work, so why not."

We were setting our motor into action, finally getting freedom from our messed-up society. Getting harsh punishments were a normal thing in households. Unless they all didn't have magic blood. Then the parents would probably love their child like a normal parent.

Chapter 2: Adding Up

After a few months of absolute toil and effort and sleepless nights of work, for both our jobs and school work, I finally decided to count the money we had earned. It was mostly from babysitting for 6 hours, everyday but we had some shoveling jobs and a little lawn mowing here and there.

My heart raced with excitement while I counted the money in my head, *74,900; 74,920; 74,940; 74,960; 74,980; 75,000; 75,020; 75,040; 75,060; 75,080; 75,100... 137,860.* I was thrilled to find out that the place we wanted was still on sale and no one had bought it yet. Maybe they forgot about the fact it was on sale. We could even hire people to help! I didn't know this was humanly possible. Okay, some nice people gave us tips (they didn't have magic by the way. Those who had magic had spoiled brats in their house. Not all of them, just most of them. Some genuinely loved their child even if they didn't have magic and were nice enough to spare us some extra money).

Haven found out there was already Wi-Fi set up there. We debated for a while for the perfect password for the Wi-Fi. I thought of, 'Sorry we don't have Wi-Fi here'. Meanwhile, Cai thought of, 'Why DO you want my Wi-Fi password?' In the end, we made a vote but I had one more vote. Cai didn't mind too much.

While talking with my friends, I forgot to tell everyone at recess about the good news. I bursted into excitement waiting for everyone after school, "GOOD

NEWS! We have more than enough to by that house and it has only been like, one or two months! Or maybe three, I'm not sure anymore."

For simple communication, I got Rose, Lydia and me smartwatches from the spare money left. Smartwatches are surprisingly cheap here. We decided to use the rest of the money for hiring workers.

Chapter 3: House Chores Picker

When we finally finished the house with help of some people we hired and some nice friend, I decided to work on the garden. I planted some flowers in the front of the house. In the backyard, it was a whole plant farm in one backyard. With pomegranate saplings, orange saplings, apple saplings, mints, cabbage, radish, carrots, tomatoes, potatoes, lemons, etc.

"That's every plant that I know," Haven looked at the transformation in our backyard.

"Same," I agreed and went inside to wash my hands free of dirt.

"Guys! We need to have chores and care of the house, you know," Rose bounced inside the house from the outdoor mini-pool we built.

"I'll cook, I am good at it and I love doing it. I'll wash the dishes too but someone needs to put it away," I said.

"Thanks, Dawn!" Rose cheered, smiling nice and big.

I announced, "And when we move in tonight, we will start calling each other a family and treat each other with respect and equality like a true family should. We will also take family pictures and if we need to and have family meetings. In case you didn't hear or forget what I said, I will announce it tomorrow when we have settled in and I will explain."

"Alright!" Lydia beamed, "I already feel like we are family!"

"I know," I smiled as well. It was time to see our plan through.

I took a piece of paper and a pencil and a pot. On the piece of paper I wrote: Sweeping and vacuuming the floor every week, doing the trash from every room every week, dusting and cleaning every room every week, grocery shopping if needed, pet feeder, laundry, watering the plants, and putting away the dishes.

I ripped the paper into separate pieces and folded them, and placed it in the pot. Cai pulled dusting and cleaning rooms every week from out of the pot. Lydia got stuck doing the trash, Rose had to do weekly sweeping and vacuuming, and Haven gladly got grocery shopping if needed.

"I'll have the last ones as well as cooking and the dishes," I said as I got pet feeder and laundry, "Is this okay with everyone?"

They all nodded, ready for some responsibilities.

"Just saying, feel free to bring your pets or animal friends if you have them," I said. Mainly because I already had a few in mind that I really wanted to ring along with me

"Okay! I know who I am going to bring. I am bringing all four of them," Haven smiled, "But I can't say I don't have weird friends. You make weird friends when you re lonely. Even if you know they aren't the best friends you might be able to find out there, it's better than being alone."

"Okay," Lydia nodded, trying not to laugh.

Chapter 4: The Move

I packed only some of my clothes into my backpack since some of it didn't fit in my backpack. I was layering clothes on me in case you were wondering. I took a spare helmet that was my size, placed it on my head, and put my backpack on and leaped on the bicycle. I knew how to ride one since there was a biking club at school that I had attended for a few years. Biking wasn't illegal here so, of course, I took the chance to learn.

A familiar stray tabby cat ran over to me with his long red fur swaying in the late-night breeze. With his emerald green eyes, he stared up at me. We knew each other quite well. I guess you could say, he understood my feelings. I talked to him a lot. Pfft, talking to a cat, how lonely are you? Very lonely, don't judge me. Like Haven said, you'll make odd friends.

"Hi Flame," I smiled, "How's Lily?"

The she-cat emerged, her golden eyes and white fur stood out in the darkness of the night. A little white cat followed. Her eyes seemed to glow brightly in the night. The stray kitten rubbed her eyes with her paw. Her golden yellow and blue eyes were absolutely stunning and the tiny cat looked around behind her mom.

"I am going somewhere else to live, want to come? I am moving there and it may take a few trips, okay?" I asked.

The tabby nodded while I was thinking of a name for the baby kitten that I just met. I thought of Light for a name or Aurora or Helios as its name. Helios sounded more like a male cat's name, so I decided to stick with Light but then I thought of Lux. I decided it would be Aurora because in my opinion, it was best, and it sounded just as lovely as the kitten was. Okay, that whole rant was totally unneeded.

They raced carefully behind me as I walked into what was supposedly my room. There was a loft bed with a desk and lamp underneath. The staircase up to my bed was built with drawers and my closet was a walk-in closet. There was a hook on my closet door for my backpack. I looked at the slide that led down to the floor from my bed. Shelves and a desk that next to where I was standing, was placed underneath my bed.

Under the slide were more shelves but for paper, pencils, files, notebooks, random objects, etc. I had one swing style chair hanging from my ceiling in one corner of the room. I also had a bean bag on the ground. In that corner, I had some bookshelves. One shelf opened like a door that led into a mini bathroom. Another corner led to the balcony. The balcony was connected to all of our rooms. I shared a bathroom with Haven. Lydia and Rose shared one, and the only boy of the group had one to himself for obvious reasons.

I raced back onto what was now my bike and with an empty backpack on my back. I headed back 'home' to make another trip.

I told my little friends, "Stay here, I'm coming back with more stuff."

I raced back to my now-old house on Rosemary's old bike, pedaling as fast as I could. I packed more clothes in backpack. The rest of them were sweaters and I pulled them over my head. *The cold ain't beating me tonight!* I snorted at the thought. I had to stuff my backpack full with my clothes. Maybe it's time to get a new backpack? Bad timing? Okay, okay, I know.

On my next trip back, I packed my hairbrushes, toothbrush, and belongings of mine. Like things I won. Including trophies, certificates, and much more.

I finally finished settling in and laid on the bed, dead still. My body ached so badly, and my muscles were extremely sore and tired from the late-night bike riding back and forth. Never once in my life had I ever made so many trips back and forth in a long distance in and uneasy terrain. I then hit the hay on my bed and snoozed for what seemed like a week but in reality, it was only 2 hours.

"Ahh!" I jerked awake. Havoc had been unleashed downstairs, waking me up.

"Who?! Who's there?!" Haven demanded holding a pot in front of her.

"Haven, can't you tell that someone is trying to sleep at like 4:36 AM?" I squinted at the digital clock, the four shifted to a nine and a one. The three turned into an eight and six and the six turned into a five through my tired eyes, "Or is it only 1:36 AM? It's too dark to be

9:35 AM. Anyway, I believe you and your pets woke me up?" I yawned, walking down the stairs. I recognized her voice.

"Oh, it's only you," Haven lowered the pot.

"I'll help you, I guess," I wandered over, still tired.

"Thanks! Take care of our new pets, Alex, Cory, Grey, and Winter. Trust me, I am not good with creative names," Haven yawned as well.

"What do you mean? You're great with names," I ambled over and then jerked back awake. Four giant adult-sized wolves sprinted at me, with what I assume was at full speed, "Ahhhhh! Why the frick do you have wolves as pets!" She didn't answer, knowing I knew dang well her answer.

I knew wolves were fast but I didn't know how fast. I was the fastest in my grade, but I don't think I could outrun four wild wolves. I ran for the back door; the only option. I dashed outside as quickly as possible.

I shouted, "Haven! Could you help me here?! Your wolves are going to kill me! Not even my pets are WOLVES!"

"No they aren't, they are just excited, you know? They are going to be guard wolves for us. Guarding things and slashing intruders are their specialties. Well, for these wolves anyhow. Dogs were domesticated from wolves," Haven chuckled, "Hey guys! Bones!"

The wolves ran over at the opposite direction they were previously running, immediately, knocking Haven down to the ground. Haven laughed and giggled as they licked her face. Lily and Flame ran over to the wolves hearing the noise.

"They seem to have already met," I told Haven.

"That's because they have, I have seen them play together. They are friends and help each other," Haven smiled.

"Huh," I said and then let silence take over the room as we worked, helping Haven get settle.

The wolves pushed the bags to the stairs, then waited for us to bring the bags up and they then pushed it into Haven's bedroom. Haven's room looked like mine but the furniture was rearranged and with a different color palate than mine.

Cai came next with a brown rabbit and a small white rabbit in his arms. The white one was called Snowball and the brown one was Mudtail. Cai had brought their little cage and their brushes and their food too. Rose brought her 2 parrots, Blueberry and Snowy. Rose brought their food and cages as well and hung them on a chain that was attached to the ceiling of her room.

Lydia brought Jimmy the hamster. Her hamster was male and golden brown in color. Then we all hit the hay. We all slept til' around 11 AM. It was such a relief that it was Sunday and not Monday. Otherwise we would be very late for school and get punished. We'd probably get cafeteria detention. We'd spend hours cleaning the cafeteria until the floor is scrubbed clean and the tables sparkled and shone (The floor is forever stained with people's vomit. The underside of the tables are covered with sticky, old, chewed gum. Gross.).

It was March 31st today. I went downstairs to make some food. I made some pancakes and the smell of blueberry pancakes with syrup and butter got everyone out of bed and coming down the stairs drooling for a taste of the pancakes.

Once everyone ate their fill, I tapped my fork on my water cup to make a small noise to get everyone's attention, "As some of you know, we will be taking pictures today, family pictures to be exact and we will do so every year to celebrate this day. We will now be known as family. As four sisters and one brother."

"Yeah!" Everyone cheered and left to dress in their best clothes.

A little while later, we all arrived at the picture spot and paid for the pictures. Everyone settled in and fit themselves into the frame. Our pets stood on our shoulders or on our head except for Winter, Alex, Cory, and Grey whom sat laid down on the side of the picture, just barely fitting in.

Today, all our hard work earned us each a phone along with its battery. You won't believe how cheap electrics are here. It's getting people to be nice to you that's expensive. While exploring the woods, I quickly found a small stream with some fish in it.

During dinner, I announced, "Alright everyone, next Saturday and Sunday will be family bonding days. I will tell you more about it on Saturday and Sunday but you may ask questions about it unless you want me to explain right now."

"It's okay," Lydia smiled, "I can wait. If you excuse me, could I pack my homework and supplies for school tomorrow?"

"For that, you don't even have to ask," I agreed, "But before you go, just to tell you, like always, we'll meet at the courtyard after school, alright?"

"Alright!" they all agreed.

"But who decided to make you the boss, Dawn?" Rose asked teasingly.

"I did," I smiled, "Because I am the 2nd oldest out of all of us, am I right, or am I right?"

"Your right!" they started laughing, rolling their eyes playfully.

Chapter 5: Mission Success

I rode my bike on the way to school the next morning with my new family of 5, including me. I saw my old house and grimaced at it with disgust, spitting at it. We reached the courtyard which was in the front of the 2 story building. The school building was in an upside down U shape. Visualize, mate, don't complain to me that you don't get it. Think 2D wise, it's not actually 2 towers with a skywalk in between. Or whatever those things are called.

In front of the courtyard, was a gate and a small row of bike stands. I handed Cai, Haven, Lydia, and Rose a lock to keep our bikes there without the worry of thievery. Mine was pure white, Haven's was pitch black, Cai's was light brown like his hair, Rose's was emerald/dark minty green, and Lydia's was sapphire blue/deep sky blue.

My combination was 253935; my lucky combination. I noticed Rosemary reaching the edge of the island from the corner of my eye. Our school is pretty close to the edge of the island. She touched her pendant and wings grew on her. She flew over the water with black and purple dragon-like wings. The scales on her wings were nice and shiny, the webbed part of her wings was silky.

I recalled a moment from a few years back when I saw Rosemary touch her pendant. Wings sprouted from her back, and markings appeared on her arm whilst she touched foreheads with an emerald colored dragon; her spirit guardian/animal. I was in a forest when it happened and she was in the sunlight of a clearing in the forest. The sunlight shined on the emerald green grass. I was in the shadows, obviously.

"Dawn!" a loud, sharp voice brought me back to reality, "You are going to be late for class and you know dang what happens if you are! Get to class right now!"

I looked up at the giant principal. He towered over me. He had that scary face people with high authority put on, not to stereotype, I promise. I gulped in fear, and saluted while saying, "Yes, Sir," then I absolutely ran for my life. Probably faster than Haven's four wolves could chase me. That's because he has the power to order the police to take me to prison for acting out of line with the other 'filth' in the world.

Once I was safe, I slowed down to a walk, thinking of my old life as I approached my classroom. Where I was always feeling invisible, I no longer felt that way. It always seemed like I was cursed into the shadows by Rosemary and her spell casting. I knew for sure she couldn't control people but it felt connected for some strange reason. It felt like it.

What was up with people hating people with no magic? It was almost like segregation version 2. We weren't even allowed to vote or have our own president or army, etc. I wanted to change it but I felt like I couldn't do anything, stranded on this island, barely seen, and with such little power. I was so small in society, I could disappear, and nothing was change. I was only a tiny neutron in comparison to the world, which could be seen as an egg. Why an egg, you ask? I have no clue, it's the first thing that popped in my mind.

When Saturday finally came around, I explained, "So, Family Bonding Day is where we connect with each other in pairs of 2. The one without someone, seen as we have 5 people and not 4 or 6, can do something they like. However, no burning the house down and stuff; the obvious. I have already made pairs for the first round. Rose and Lydia, and Cai and I."

Haven went upstairs to start playing games while Rose and Lydia decided to do something outside together. They walked outside and closed the door to make sure no flies would fly in and stuff. Cai and I did arts and crafts and made rings. We each made one for each other. Nothing weird is going on, I promise. You ask me about it and you'd frickin' **better** pray to make it out alive.

Cai picked a clear white plastic jewel and took some sliver and slightly melted it to a malleable state. He then shaped the sliver into the shape of a ring with sliver spiraling around the gem. It was connected to the bottom spiral. The top and bottom ring made a circle If you looked at it from the top or bottom. Then he made a matching piece and place it a little bit higher than the first one.

I was super impressed at the ring he made. I got a rectangle piece of fake gold, a chisel, and a small hammer and carved his name with hearts on each end.

We made rings for the others and later gave it to them. They liked it, thankfully. We spent quite a bit of time making them.

I made Haven's ring; it was made with a dark black iron piece. On the underside, it said ~`*Haven*'~

I went fishing near the spring with Lydia, and gardening with Rose, finally with Haven, I taught her outdoor cooking.

"You guys know how many people on the island have weaponry to defend themselves. Billions of people," I brought up.

"Yeah," Lydia looked up.

I said, "We should too, for self-defense of course. It's not illegal. No one cares if we have weapons, so we should have some for self-defense."

The next day, we spent the whole day making weaponry for self-defense. Rose made nunchucks, a sword, throwing stars that stayed in a bag on her hip, and katanas that sat behind each shoulder. Lydia had a spear that was placed behind her back. She had a sword, a bow and a quiver of arrows, and a dagger. Haven had a sword, a bow and a quiver of arrows, and a scythe. Cai had a sword; a bo, a Japanese staff; throwing stars; and a double sided sword.

I had a sword that was held on my waist with a belt. I also had a spear and staff behind my left shoulder next to each other. Behind my right shoulder was a quiver of arrows that had a strap for my bow. I had some throwing stars and kunai knives. The perks of having a babysitting job. You gain a lot of friends in different fields, including people in the blacksmithing industry and people in the weaponry industry.

I made a few targets and bought fighting machines to practice. We practiced as often as we could between jobs until we could master self-defense and attacks in case we needed it.

We sat in the living room chatting while watching a good movie, when a knock came at the door. It was louder than the sound effects from the movie and shattered my eardrums. Someone was clearly pissed off, and for what reason, I don't know.

"I'll get it," I paused the movie as they patiently waited for me.

I opened to door, annoyed by their rude knocking. I was about to curse at whoever it was. I opened the door and froze.

Chapter 6: 5 Golden Letters of Honor

"You!" I burst in anger as I spat, "Get away from here! How'd you even find us?" Seriously? That's the best I could have come up with to let them know I didn't want them here?

"Rosemary is dying, you are going to be our only child soon, please come back," they pleaded.

"Please," I said sarcastically, rolling my eyes in the process. So **now** they want me, "Now you notice me? You didn't notice anything I did for you guys but thank god I left home. Did it take you that long to notice I stopped coming home every day? What kind of parent's are you? I have found myself a new and better family and now you want me back to fulfill your hearts? Please, like I will."

"Please, we need you now," Mom pleaded and begged. She face changed into a threatening look. The look I never once fought back or talked back against, "And who are you to talk back aganst authority?! I'm your parent! I birthed you and carried you for nine months. I gave you your life, isn't it a few years too soon to be talking back at me?! I have magic in my blood, so I'm in charge here, I have status!"

"Not happening, I'm not going home," I smirked, feeling strong for once, "Go back to that dump. Look, I even got a family photo to secure my place here. Not that it proves much. I just makes me sound like a whiny brat. Figures you haven't noticed I wasn't there for a single family picture. Wouldn't notice if I disappeared now huh?"

"Yeah. And in this family, we all support each other and care for each other," Cai hissed, his ears sticking flat in annoyance, baring his fangs and he stuck his middle finger in their face.

I agreed, "You were never there when I need you guys the most, like the burglar thing two weeks before my 4th birthday and wouldn't let me sleep with you guys but let Rosemary let sleep with you guys and gave me a cot that smell like BARF!"

"What burglar thing? Is it when the burglar came in your room and stole Rosemary's things?" Haven asked.

"Yeah," I turned to Haven then returned to glaring at my biological parents and spat, "I had to sleep with a broken window for years. I never felt safe whereas Rosemary had all the security. I was casted completely into her shadows. I hate it!"

"While Rosemary was your main interest and light! Your sun! You surrounded her with love! Not me! I'm a filthy nobody in your eyes!" I continued, the rest of us all glared at them.

"Okay look, we are staying here until you come with us. I'm being nice instead of burning this place down," Mom said than asked, "What's your Wi-Fi password?"

"Sorry, we don't have Wi-Fi here," I recited with a big smirk and then mentally broke into laughter, watching her fall right into the plan.

I slammed the door in their faces but the ear-shattering knocks came again and I kicked them both in the shin but they were persistent. Maybe that's where I get my own persistence from.

I drew my sword and stuck it in front of their faces glaring. I was about to be cringy, but don't mind me, "Go scram before I start saying some words as nasty as you guys. Pardon my language."

"Yeah!" Haven hissed, siding with me.

I yelled at my parents, sword at their throat, "I am practically casted into the shadows! You don't care about me! If you want a child, just make another!"

They left so fast, they dropped their phones and I plopped them in the trash. I mean, if someone stuck swords at your necks, you'd probably run too, stubborn or not. But now I'm wondering how the heck are they scared of some threats? *Hm, maybe it's my threatening aura.* I smiled creepily, enjoying it.

Later that day, the mailman arrived with 5 golden envelopes for each of us. Inside was a letter written with a golden sheet of paper:

Dear Dawn H.,

We would be pleased to inform that you will be selected to start the Magic Academy on the Magic Island for a new start and chance at life. I will greet you upon your arrival from the carrier men. I will most likely greet you with a, "May I temporarily set you on fire or burn you?" which is personally one of my favorite things to say.

If you decide to leave, I won't be very happy if you come back. I would wish for you guys to appreciate this offer. There are clubs you can join if you would like to join a club. The school doesn't have uniforms but the mascot is a fire fox which is after me since I'm part fire fox, and the school colors are red and orange like a fire fox.

You will attend the same classes as the other selected 4 which I believe are your friends. It is a boarding school and you may go back at the end of the year and during breaks. You will start school one week after you arrive and settle in.

You will be picked up on 5/1/20 at 11:00 AM Pacific Time. See you there and hopefully you become great friends with our best students even the one that may die. Our top student, Rosemary. She is great, from what I've seen.

Rosemary, is honest. She is also our long lasting number 1 student, and a student favorite of the student body. If you return a book late, you will get a fee of 5 dollars. If you hurt someone, you will get detention. If you spill your food, you are on clean duty for the whole Cafeteria. If you lie, you get suspended

Sincerely,
Prince Changle of Magic Island

"Rosemary?!" Lydia spat as she saw her letter.

Second place was Lydia's deadly older brother that killed her parents and was trying to kill Lydia. 3rd place was Rose's brother. Rose's family tried to hunt her down once but Lydia saved Rose in time. 4th place was Fern, who actually cared to Haven when they left this island. Slay, Fern.

"This Prince dude forgot to put a period on mine!! And he can't seem to organize paragraphs!" I sighed, "This letter is defective!"

"Yet again, everyone is defective," Haven shrugged.

Chapter 7: Cursed

I had finished packing my clothes and left the house filled with spider traps and mouse traps in case spiders and mice invited themselves into our humble abode. I knew the special path to get around the traps including one that that would send people and insects to our tiny prison cell for insects, rodents, and humans alike.

"Are you ready? I'm going to carry you across. After all, you can't fly, can you?" asked a carrier man holding my luggage and me in his arms. He was clearly mocking me. I call it.

"Yep, I guess so, but you're kinda rude, ya' know," I tried to breathe but the man held me way too tight for my liking, "Help, you're squishing me too hard, idiot! I need to breathe!"

As soon as I arrived, I saw the face of the spoiled brat that Mom and Dad's raised. She was greeting our arrival and was leading us to Prince Changle. She was supposed to hold my arm but I refused.

"Cut it out!" I yelled in a bad mood and slapped the arm away with a loud crack. I can't say my hand didn't sting afterwards.

"Sheesh, you didn't have to hit me," she rolled her eyes like she was innocent. As if she was.

We entered the extravagant school building, Prince Changle gave her a smile and gave her a high-five. I was yet again going to be in her shadows. Wonderful, I'm really starting to take a liking to this place. I'm totally not rolling my eyes right now. I really don't know what you are talking about.

"May I temporarily set you on fi-?" Changle started talking

I snapped, interrupting him, "Could you hurry up with the prep-talk before I am IN the ground with a tombstone that says, 'Prince Changle let her die of impatience.'?"

"Uhh, what?" Changle asked clearly confused.

I looked at Haven standing next to me. She rolled her eyes and mumbled, "Hurry up already. I'm dying here. **We're** dying here."

"Huh?" Changle asked still not getting it.

"Never mind, just hurry up, will ya, we don't have all day. Time doesn't come back, you know," I sighed.

"Alright, geez," Changle took out a piece of paper, "Your schedule."

Changle then gave us each a separate piece of paper that said our ID, locker number. Mine was my lucky number combination, 253934 and my locker number was 1, which apparently turns out to be the worst locker possible.

I walked almost a mile to finally reach locker 1. As well as the rest of us. Cai got 2, Haven got 3, Lydia got 4, and Rose got 5, so of course our lockers would be close by. In addition, my locker was ruined and it seemed like it was kicked all the time.

The lock didn't even work, it didn't even open at all. It wouldn't budge but when I kicked it, it smacked me right on the face then closed again.

"Need help?" Cai asked.

"Yeah," I frowned, "This locker won't open properly."

I watched doubtfully as he put in my password and easily opened it. My mouth held open in shock, how could he do it and I couldn't. I looked inside my locker. It was filled with gum and cobwebs and spiders. A shelf in it was broken and hanging from one rusty nail. I accidently poked myself on shattered glass from god knows where. The bottom, we don't talk about it. Or about the mold and mushrooms growing on the side. Where did it come from anyway? Narnia? The monster in my closet? Someone please explain.

When I explored my classroom and went to meet my teachers, I had to sit on the bedrock hard cold ground with a cardboard box as a desk. Once, during the day, when I was watching others, I left to use the restroom, and when I came back, my seat, which was bad enough, had become a sea of Legos and the teacher didn't even care and just smiled and forced me to sit down.

When I went to my dorm, which was obviously old, I was seriously pissed. There were dents and missing corners and walls of the dorm. The windows were broken and the window shade was in tatters. I found a hole in the ground and the wall in one area. The balcony door was broken and I almost stepped into death. A few seconds more and my life would be flashing before my guys. Given the fact I doubt I'd survive a fall from the ninth floor. Why?! The balcony wasn't even there! Why did I have all the bad things happening to me! Stupid luck I have! I nearly missed some broken glass and some rusted nails on the ground. I'd really like to file a complaint! Right now! Please!

I heard voices outside my dorm. I assumed it was on my level, in the ninth story in the dorm building. I was living on level nine which was my common room chamber.

Rosemary told her friends, Celeste and Maranda, "I mean, that little devil of a smarty pants got The Room, the haunted room, can you believe it?"

"Totally, she is so weak, like she doesn't even have a drop of magic blood. Not even an atom. She doesn't even deserve to be here," Celeste laughed.

Cai popped out of nowhere and hissed, "Don't you frog-danggit talk about her that way, idiot! You're more pathetic than winning a medal for a breathing contest."

"So? We have all the rights of freedom and you guys don't. We can always send you back with one word. And watch your language with us. You have no right to speak with such profanity," Maranda stuck her nose in Cai's face, "Or we could cut of your tail and ears or maybe even your head. What do you say?"

Cai stood, tucked his ears and tails in and shoved them down the stairs with a small push, "You're just all talk. You okay, Lil' Dawn?"

"Yeah," I turned red, "But you know that I am only like 6 months younger than you, I'm not little."

"Whatever. I'm still taller than you," Cai smiled, "I'm sure your room. It's not haunted."

"You are only taller by like 2 inches. Thanks for making Rosemary 'disappear'. You're the best. She probably has a broken ankle now," I started laughing and hugged him. Again, don't think too much about it. Move on. We were a real family now. I could sincerely feel it, "But you'll get in trouble."

"Friends will do that for their family. Family will suffer the consequences to help their loved ones," Cai waved at me as he left to go to his room.

I turned to the old, half destroyed four poster bed with ripped curtains. The straw filled pillow and blanket was as uncomfortable as it looked. The mattress was filled with what seemed like live insects crawling all around inside. Nonetheless, I sat on it.

I gulped in fear as a gray-ish figure floated over. The figure spoke, "You look like you've seen a ghost."

I sat off to the side of te bed trying not to scream in fear. What was it? Slowly, one by one, more like her appeared. All around me and some hovering above me.

This time I screamed, "Ahhh!"

Haven and Cai heard my scream and ran to my room. My sword and weapons were on the other side of the room. I walked backwards going through them, so I could get to my weapons. I drew my sword and attacked but it just went right through them.

"We're spirits, silly, don't you know what spirits are?" the first figure asked. The figure was likely a woman.

Haven, Cai, and I all shook our heads like clueless idiots, "Nope."

"What's the flipping difference between a ghost and a spirit anyway?" I asked.

"A ghost is usually less civilized than us spirits," the lady replied. I held back a laugh at that comment.

"Oh my, let me guess, Prince Changle brought you here from the non-magic island?" a man holding the lady's hand guessed, "The name's Mr. Forest and my wife here is Mrs. Forest."

"Nice to meet you?" I said unsurely and awkwardly. I slowly walked out of the room, "Later!"

Chapter 8: A Long Held Secret

The next week, I found out that Celeste, Maranda, and Rosemary were all in my class but they were doing something, when I came to see what class would be like. I knew all the answers but they were struggling a bit. I was never noticed except by my friends or the spirits that floated around my room. My hand held up high in the air.

No one chose me and then I shouted angrily, "Excuse me, but I believe I exist?!"

"Whatever," the teacher ignored me.

"I am going to the bathroom!" I shouted, aggravated.

"You don't have to say it, filth, just go," my teacher, Mrs. Dante spat, "Anyone else?"

I left to go to the bathroom just before Celeste, Maranda, and Rosemary raised their hand. I went to wash my hands as I looked at the scars that I received from when Rosemary threw knives at me when I was 3. I sighed, looking at them. Sadly enough, if you had status, this was allowed. With status, pretty much everything was legal. If you didn't have status, tough luck getting out of jail.

The three girls entered the bathroom with a full case of the giggles. They held their fists up and knives. I didn't have my sword with me and I slowly crawled away but bonked the wall. Not that this isn't natural behavior towards people without magic. We didn't have rights, power, nor the right to speak up aganst society. And I was only a small dot in the non-magic society. I also wasn't normally someone to back away and cower like that.

They threw stuff at me on Rosemary's cue and choked me to the wall and punched me. It's not like they worried about repercussions. The only thing a cop would do if they were passing by, would just look. *Just breathe in and breathe out, this isn't the first time.*

I was way too hurt to even get up so I just lay there hoping someone would help me but instead people just stepped over me.

Mrs. Forest found me and carried me to the hospital tower. A nurse, named Samantha, didn't even want help me because I didn't have magic so Mrs. Forest carried me back to my room herself.

Cai noticed me and asked, "What happened?"

"Door swung on me multiple times," I lied.

After I was back in my room, Mrs. Forest said, "Now, now, what is the use to lie to him. You know you need his help, right?"

"Yeah," I replied, "But the girls will kill me if I do. AND them which is why I don't want to tell them. Showing them would be no different. I don't want them to hurt my family."

I took a warm bath and Mrs. Forest took care of my wounds for me.

"Thank you Mrs. Forest," I smiled as she replaced my bed with a new one that was nice and comfy.

"You're welcome dearie," she smiled.

Chapter 9: Why Did You Lie to Me?!

One month passed and through studying, people with no magic, later could get magic. I was jumping up and down inside. Rosemary wasn't very pleased. Nor were her friends that hurt me daily.

"What did I ever do to them?" I grumbled to Mr. Forest.

"I don't know but they surely hate you. However, us spirits will help you through it, we'll do everything to keep you on your feet and I mean it figuratively," Mrs. Forest gave me a hug, one that I could actually feel since I would keep going through her if I tried to hug her.

"Yeah," Mr. Forest appeared on my right.

One month later, my friends all had magic and knew I was very clumsy and kept 'falling' and getting 'hit' by doors. Lydia had water magic, Rose had earth type while Haven had dark and Cai had health. Meanwhile, I still didn't have magic. I still couldn't understand why. Maybe it's not in my genes. I'm not meant to. I'm meant to be a failure in society.

Nothing changed for me. When Changle had announced when we came, "I hope none of you go back to that island, it has been a pleasure to meet you."

I had told him that very day, "Not really to me," Not like he'd know why.

It had been a month since then. Haven, Cai, Rose, and Lydia all had pendants to temporarily have wings. I was in the bathroom but Haven was already in there and I didn't know. She's sneaky like that. Celeste, Maranda, and Rosemary geared up on me. Haven froze all of us and the only thing we could do was talk.

"*A-hem* I spy with my little eyes, a liar," Haven glared at me, "How long has this been going on?"

"Since I-I f-first got h-hurt," I trembled, sorta scared, due to the look she was giving me. Okay, I was really scared. I'm a stubborn idiot, you guys know this. I don't have the balls to just admit something like that.

"Well, sorry, I don't want to live with a liar. I am out of the family. A family member doesn't lie to another," Haven frowned, narrowing her eyebrows.

My heart shattered in a million pieces, tears rolled down my cheeks. She unfroze me and I ran up to my room in tears, laying in my bed, not even getting up to eat or drink, just lying there in my wet bed sheets covered in my tears. I was just trying to protect them, dammit. Why does life hate me? The place I worked so hard to build, ended, just like that. It was my own fault, I knew it. She easily felt betrayed, and I made her feel betrayed.

Then, things got worse, Haven told the rest of them and left me to be with Haven and I was alone, once again. They reformed a new family without me. Mrs. Forest tried to get me to eat but I didn't feel like it. I felt like throwing the ring that Cai had made while we were still a family on Family Bonding Day out the window, on Cai's happy little face down below with Haven and the rest of my 'family'. I felt so betrayed.

I pulled my ring off when Mrs. Forest said, "Stop, don't do it, you'll probably regret it. Plus, you like him don't you? That might be the last memory you have of him."

I put it back on, a little red, holding myself back from lunging at her. I warned ya'll. I then asked, "That's none of your concern. Why does the bad stuff always have to happen to me anyway?"

"Beats me," Sarah, Mr. and Mrs. Forest's daughter shrugged, "But I would love to help you through it. I know you lied for a reason, a good reason."

"Not really," I sighed.

"C'mon!" Sarah dragged me away and placed a plate food in front of me, "You need to eat or you will starve."

I ate as slow as a slug or snail could go, whereas Sarah gulped her food down, but was still careful about her table manners.

"Look!" Sarah pointed, "These are all the people who have slept here, they all died, but we have protection spells in hopes you wouldn't die. And so your picture won't be on here. We try not to have people in this room die but it just keeps happening."

I looked around and spotted a girl just like her and pointed, "Is that you?"

"Yeah, I died because of a toilet in the school. I was shoved down it as a prank, a deadly prank. The people who shoved me down tried to even flush the toilet," Sarah sighed and then pointed the two people above her picture, "That's my mom and dad. I hate toilets by the way. Hey, want to be my friend?"

"I think she is more than a friends now," Mrs. Forest floated over, "More like family."

"Family?!" I my brightened a little.

"Yes, part of our family," Mr. Forest joined Mrs. Forest.

"Yay!" Sarah smiled and hugged me, "I've always wanted a sister, a sister like you."

Pretty soon, I was smiling again but I still couldn't forget Cai, Haven, Lydia, and Rose. I mean, they were part of my first real family.

Chapter 10: Angels and Demons

I woke up with 2 feathery wings on my back. I checked on the Forest Family and they had wings too.

I asked them, "What's up with the wings?"

"It's national Angel and Demon month. For a month, the island is basically Heaven and Hell. Heaven for the angels, Hell for the demons. There are different rules like demons must sin and angels must be saints. It's a tradition past down from queen and king to queen and king," Sarah was proud to be an angel, "But we don't choose which we are, Changle's mom does. She is currently the ruler of heaven."

My head was literally spinning with confusion.

Sarah continued after eating a strawberry, "Changle's mom can banish people from Heaven. Changle's dad controls Hell but he can't do anything except making sure that the demons are in order."

"Oh?" I was still learning about the culture here, which was very different than on the non-magic island, so don't judge me.

At breakfast, when I went to sit with Lydia, Rose, Cai, and Haven, but they moved away from me. I was alone in one table. I was in a black, cyan, and pink jacket, and dark grey shorts over black pants.

At lunch, an announcement came, "Will Dawn H. please report to the office, I repeat, will Dawn H. please come to the office, NOW!"

I tensed at the demand, getting up from my seat. People shouted 'Oooh! Someone's in trouble~!' and stuff like that. I walked to the office, wondering *what had I done wrong?* I then remembered I had wings but I couldn't really use them. I could lift off the floor slightly but not much and I usually fell face flat on the floor.

"You hurt her, didn't you?" Changle's mom had zero tolerance on violence. Towards those with magic of course, "Poor Rosemary, she is our best student and she is your KIN!"

"I didn't do anything!" I cried out, anger boiled hotter under my skin by the second. Defending myself is something I just do, even if I shouldn't, "I was just eating breakfast."

"Are you saying our Rosemary is lying?!" Changle's mom demanded, "She never lies! And don't talk back to me like that, filth."

"We see about Rosemary lying," Changle mumbled and said out loud, "I guess, I have never asked her about anything so I don't really know."

"You may go now, Rosemary," Changle's mom said.

Then Rosemary exited the room. Changle saw Rosemary wash the make-up of her face and watched her smirk.

"I will call you after dinner to decide your punishment, devil," Changle's mom grumbled.

Changle ran up to me and whispers, "I'm sorry, I know you are wrongly accused."

"I-it's okay," I grumbled.

During my free time, I got the hang of flying until. I was to Hell for the rest of the month. I sat alone, unable to fly with chains on my wings. I was sitting in the dark place that had fire in the cracks of paths and lava all over the place, all alone. My, isn't this deja vu.

Chapter 11: Angels Are Devils

"Hey," A boy walked over, "What's a pretty gal like you doing here?"

"Unfairly blamed," I didn't want to talk about it.

"Oh," the boy frowned, "That's rude. Can't Changle's mom tell that it was a fib? Or whatever happened didn't happen?"

"No, but Changle did. Changle's mom didn't listen to him, I guess," I lay on the fiery grass and ground. On the bright side, it couldn't kill you. On the minus side, it's frickin' hot.

The boy introduced himself, "I am Valor (pronounced like Valerie but you cut off the end), you?"

"Dawn H. Dawn Heathens," I let out a smile.

We became great friends. He also had a crush on someone. Valor was in high school and this was his second to last year in high school. A junior at his school.

I even got Valor and his crush closer. I was of course playing the embarrassing matchmaker. Their relationship was secured and I squealed when I dared him to kiss his crush. I of course, don't regret a thing. I was playing with Valor and Bri, Valor's crush, at the border and I spotted Cai.

"Do you know him?" Valor asked.

"Yes," I replied.

Bri held Valor arm, "And I have my boyfriend."

"What does that have to do with anything?" I asked, confused. Bri just shrugged and we left it at that.

I was talking with Valor and Bri about some show they made about living life as a demon in June called Demon Days.

"H-hey," Cai smiled at me awkwardly.

I wasn't in the mood to smile to him. Especially when he left me, just because I lied to keep him safe, not just my own safety. He didn't get it. Yet again, he only heard one side of the story.

I just said to him flatly, "What?"

With this, Celeste, Rosemary, Maranda, Haven, Changle, Lydia, and Rose walked over and Rosemary sneered, "Did you know, devils can't even fly, nor are they allowed to even start a conversation with an angel, right?! Only angels can."

"So don't expect us not to fail, "saints", or should I call sinners. Which one of you blamed Dawn to Hell?! You call everyone with magic saints when it isn't June, but when it's June, then only you angels are called saints!" Valor yelled, "Angels like you are really Demons! You guys place plastic masks to try to be perfect!"

"Please, you guys can't even do magic because you guys caused unforgivable sins that sent you guys here and took your magic and flying ability away. It's obvious, only us good Magicals can fly," Maranda, Celeste, and Rosemary then retorted.

Bri than shouted and shot them a glare, "But got we didn't do anything, why?! It's just unjust! You guys are so one sided. Tsk."

I then joined in with my hands, wings, and feet in chains, "And that's what you call fair?!"

Rosemary scowled, "You know that life ain't fair sometimes, right? Drill it into your head already. You should know this."

"Only angels can be saints and that's that!" Maranda snickered.

"But we try to be like you, you guys can't seem to see it! We all have our flaws, deal with it!" Valor, Bri, and I all argued.

I sighed. I was too tired of this. I don't think I doubted myself or hesitate to say what I did, "Look, I know I don't belong here, nor with any of you, I am just a loner with no magic and I always will. I am tired of being in Rosemary's shadow, I am going back."

"Back where?" Changle was alert.

"Back home," I said with a hiss and growled, speaking in a threatening, low tone, "Demons steal? That gives me a head start. Stupid rules will be used aganst you. Am I fitting in your rules now? Am I good for you now? Well tell me, am i?"

I jumped on a motorcycle and inserted a stolen key, and drove off full speed to the beach. Changle, Cai, Haven, Lydia, and Rose had to rent motorcycles and parked behind my motorcycle as I stole a jet ski from the beach and drove off to the distance.

Changle demanded all of them fly over but once they got to the ocean, they would turn normal (the angel stuff) so Changle had them touch their pendants.

I was already back at the house my 'family' built. It still had a lot of my clothes there anyway. Cai had called me through my phone but I ignored it completely and declined the call. I was terribly upset.

How come I live a life of lies and trouble? Why did they have to leave? How come everyone had to turn against me? Was it some curse or spell or did Heaven really turn against me? I can't do anything right. I did lie... but for a good purpose. I thought, raging mentally.

A bang at the door rang brought me to reality, "OPEN UP, Dawn!"

I eyes were puffed from the crying. I opened the door, "Who are you looking for?"

Chapter 12: A True Family

I saw an angry Changle half-brainwashed by Celeste at my door step. So angry in fact, he looked like he was about to bust the house into tiny pieces. If he did, I'd bust HIM into tiny atoms and avenge my fallen house.

Changle shouted, "I said you gotta stay at the Magic Island. Are you not thankful I gave you a new chance?!"

"Not really, because it brought back terrible memories of my past and I didn't like that feeling. The family that I joined with me left me because I lied to protect them from your so-called god, Rosemary! I would've been better here. Where I don't feel like crap with Rosemary showing me up" I yelled in his face and then ran upstairs to my room and locked it. Pardon my language, I'm just gunna say it now. I say it a lot, I know. However, pardon my language. Whatever manages to come out of my mouth.

Flame hissed at Changle. Changle screamed, not knowing what a cat was.

Meanwhile Cai walked through the traps patting Changle's shoulder, "You don't know her past very well, do you."

Aurora and Lily laid next to me worryingly and Aurora tried to entertain me with things related to what I liked like basketball, ice skating, the drums, and karate. Aurora rolled my basketball to me and I smiled weakly.

Sitting in someone's shadow wasn't the greatest thing in the world. In fact, it sucked. I wanted to ruin Rosemary's life, ruin her reputation but then, it would be really mean of me to ruin her life and reputation.

Changle barged in through the balcony and grabbed onto my hair, "You don't just do that, young lady!"

"I can," I shouted, "Because I have the right to leave, unless you want to use me as a slave because I have no magic, I never will listen to you! I would never be so called Mrs. Perfect, my biological sister!"

Changle held on tight. Cai told Changle to go and said to me, "I know it's hard. Your past, I mean. Look, I am sorry for leaving the family, I didn't know you were trying to protect us. I just thought you were just lying for Rosemary's reputation, you were just trying to do what you thought was right, I rejoin the family and I won't ever leave. Cross my heart and hope to die."

Cai held me in my arms in a hug as I said, "But why does it have to be me? Why is it me without magic, when you guys have magic? Plus, if I could, I would ruin Rosemary's reputation and life like she ruined mine. And don't hope to die."

Haven walked over, "I sorry, I am coming back to the family. I know your past quite well. I remember hearing the chaos when I was 3, I heard a racket in your house on Christmas and I listened in. I saw you do everything you could do to get noticed but Rosemary was noticed every small thing she did, good or bad alike and they went on a celebration without you. I didn't know that behind your lie, was a good intention. I just felt so betrayed, I wasn't thinking rationally about what you could be thinking."

One by one, they apologized to me but Changle was a bit more headstrong like Rosemary, Maranda, and Celeste. I didn't care and smiled, tears drying. Aurora was happily rolling at the reunion. We took another family picture that day, June 19th. Thankfully it was the last day of school and we all decided stayed here to do our chores, and enjoy time together again.

"I don't care that daddy used to rage and yell at you or that I made that nasty scar on your face and no one took you to the hospital. Lookie there, lookie there, I think her face is infected by the knife I used. Let you on a little secret, the knife was used to cut raw meat," Rosemary taunted sticking out her tongue suddenly.

"That's enough!" Cai stood up in anger, "My power senses there is no infection what so ever. Nowhere on her body is there an infection! And we all know you are a liar."

"She has the cooties, watch out! It's really sickening watching someone think they are our level. Just because you gained magic doesn't mean you are the same as us," Rosemary snickered.

I stomped up to her, unable to contain my anger and spat, pulling her clothes towards me, "What do you have against me, what have I ever done, huh?! Nothing! That's what, but yet you decided to ruin my life! Trying to get me killed, aren't you?! Because you are close to your goal! You bring back so many terrible memories. I sit in your shadows all the time! It's time that I say, I HAVE HAD ENOUGH!!! AND MAYBE I'LL SLAUGHTER YOU FIRST, IN COLD BLOOD!!!!!" My words became threats. Saying I was mad, would be an understatement. I was more than pissed.

Rosemary looked frighten but then regained her cool, "Says the stupid one that never gets noticed!"

"Says the one who couldn't even spell the word cat a few years back!" it was my time to insult that fat ego of hers. And I wanted to insult it nice real good.

"Just wait until karma gets you!" Changle stuck out his tongue at me, "I can't wait."

"Maybe I'll scare the pants off you, drag you to hell where you fruckin' belong. I'll laugh my butt off when I slice your pathetic little throat open. I'll watch you die in pain and agony and I'll the last person you see before you never come back," I drew my sword, pissed. That was more of an empty threat. A threat's a threat, but I wasn't actually going to go that far. However, I'm afraid you don't know what it's like, so don't you dare judge me.

"Haha!" You think you are allowed to do that?" Celeste laughed, "And for those threats, we could place you in jail. However, we are nice people."

"Nice? Not at all. As whether I think I'll be allowed to do that, yes!" I said confidently.

"Too bad!" Changle smirked and then recited, "Rules of the magic island, fit in stupid! Good girls don't fight, and gotta be like them and wear high heels and dresses, or be a disgusting loser. Unless you are Rosemary and you are an exception."

"That's on you because I don't live there," I smiled, "Say, good girls don't fight? I am both mentality and psychically fighting of my rights. If heaven turns its back on me, that means I am a bad girl but if good girls don't fight, then I am not a good girl then am I. However, frankly, I don't care. Heavens already turned on me long ago."

"Go be useful and put on some girl clothes fit for the Magic Island and a pair of high heels," Maranda hypocritically mocked me.

"Oh really, now," I said and kicked Maranda in the shin as hard as I thought she could bear, "I could go harder, ya know? I don't have to wear high heels, but either way, I can kick you a billion times harder on a whim if I wanted to!"

They left annoyed, tired of trying to make me stay at the Magic Island. Cai made food for me and Haven did the laundry, and Lydia and Rose fed our pets, all for me and I smiled, a smile filled with pure joy.

We were a true family. When Changle left, he was no longer controlled and not completely sure what he did.

Chapter 13: Getting Ready for a Birthday

Summer was awesome! We spent time as a family and even had adventures together while camping this summer. It was the first time I've ever gone camping, since I was left alone in the house when my parents took Rosemary on camping trips.

Lydia had been camping before her brother killed her parents and now her brother was hunting for her, dead or alive. People don't know where he is, he could be anywhere. Lydia, Cai, Haven, and Rose together, used magic to make the building only visible to us but it was still our territory. Cai's birthday was coming up and the rest of us came up with a surprise party plan for Cai with the rest of us.

"He's not going to suspect a thing, is he?" Haven wondered aloud.

"He might but hopefully he wouldn't. He is taking a walk out to explore nature. He said he is coming back at noon," I smiled, it felt so good to plan this for Cai's birthday. A smile bubbled up from inside me.

"Let's buy the new school supplies and gifts for Cai's birthday!" Lydia was getting excited, but did her best not to show it.

"Yeah!" Rose shouted, a smile carving itself on her face.

I gave them each a small list of school supplies to find for the 5 of us. My present for Cai was a portable first aid kit. My reason for it, was that he was into the medical field. Haven got medical books for Cai to read.

We all pretty much based our presents around interests he had.

At night, we quickly and neatly wrapped the presents. I was too tired to realize that I had planned that party for tomorrow. I didn't know that today was already August 9th. I made a red velvet cake for him with words written on it.

When Cai walked in the door after a babysitting job and turned on the lights with a string gimmick on the door handle I set up. We popped out of our hiding places for a traditional surprise birthday party.

He screamed, in a funny high-pitched girl voice, "Ahh! Oh, it's just you g—"

"Happy birthday!" We all shouted.

Cai's eyes popped open in shock. Surely he didn't expect the classic suprise. When he regained composure, he used his nose and smelled the sweet aroma of triple chocolate cookies, red velvet and white chocolate brownies and red velvet cake, was wafting in the air, Cai ambled to the kitchen, mouth drooling for some sweets.

In the dining room, I placed the cake on the table. There, a banner said, 'Happy birthday!' in bright pink. I placed 13 candles on the cake and lit the candles. We sang happy birthday and Cai blew out the candles.

"Woo!" Haven hooted, "What did you wish for?"

"Don't say it! Don't you frickin' say it, sir!" Rose waved her hands in Cai's face, "They say that if you say it, it won't come true!"

We all laughed, talking about good times we have had as a family so far. We had a good time although we had only been a family for half a year, but that was good enough to keep me happy.

"And remember that bird dropping a random comb on Haven's head and bird droppings on mine?" Lydia asked, laughing, "Disgusting but interesting."

"Yeah!" Rose giggled.

"And the flying toothbrush at night?" Cai reminded.

"You did it!" We all laughed and launched for him teasingly.

We all slept well that night with memories that would forever stay in our hearts. Oh, sorry, was that cheesy? Suck it up, buttercup.

Chapter 14: Back There

We were heading back to Magic Island and I wasn't excited. People say that Cai, Haven, Lydia, and Rose would be switching lockers, but I wouldn't. I stayed in the same old dorm I had last school year. My friends--family stayed in the same dorm they were in last year as well. So I wasn't completely alone, I suppose.

Cai opened my locker for me all the time since it wouldn't open for me. When I first got back to the school, I kicked my locker open and I screamed as loud as I could. I assumed that China could hear me all the way from here in Washington in this alternate universe. The alternate universe China could hear me, not the non-magical universe could hear me. Thing is, we know we live in an alternate universe from everyone else in the real world. Maybe I could escape there someday.

There was a giant tarantula smiling wickedly at me with a giant cobweb. It was unnaturally large and possibly the size of my face.

A voice rang behind me, "Dawn! I missed you so much! Oh, that spider. I'll get rid of it. Rosemary put it there to prank you."

"Sarah!" I turned around.

"Who is she hugging?" Cai asked.

"I am starting to wonder is she is going crazy," Haven used her magic, "Oh, it's a spirit. Only whoever the spirit cares for can see the spirit. I am guessing because she sleeps in the quote-quote haunted dorm."

"You mean you can't see her?" I asked, surprised.

"Well," Lydia said, "We could but we need magic to see it."

"Yeah," Sarah explained to me.

I nodded in to show I understood my friends. I unpacked my things in my dorm and I found that the bed was new like the other beds and Sarah smiled.

Sarah boasted about her amazing parents, "It was Mommy's idea and Daddy built it. I choose the fabrics and all. Plus, we put rails and nets where you could fall."

"Thanks!" I smiled and hugged her and her family. My black, pink, and cyan jacket fell down by my waist behind me. On the inside, I had a plain white t-shirt.

"We fixed the lights too," Mrs. Forest smiled.

"Wow, I didn't notice that it flickered but thank you Mr. and Mrs. Forest!" I noticed Mr. Forest walking in and smiled.

"Our little girl, did you and your friends rejoin the family?" Mr. Forest hugged me.

"It's nice to see all of you guys again, really. I am hoping I'll get magic this year and wouldn't be a person with no magic anymore! And best of all, my friends and I are a family again! We also surprised Cai with a birthday party," I smiled big at the thought, my words coming out all over the place.

"We hope you will get your magic this year as well. Congrats getting back together as a family," Mr. Forest neatened my bed.

I woke up early the next morning, ready for a new start and turn over a new leaf. Turns out the only difference was a glaring, callous look, and a rude Changle. Well, I guess I couldn't really expect him to know what I did, since it was a blur for him. Celeste controlled him and he was mad at me for randomly leaving. There were a few more people from the non-magical island this time around.

"You should be glad I came back even though I didn't want to," I took a seat.

Changle lightened up, "Whatever."

"Enjoy the spider?" Rosemary giggled.

I glared at her in disgust and shivered, "You are the only real spider here, and your ugliness feels like legs crawling up my spine."

"OI!!! YOU TAKE THAT BACK RIGHT NOW! YOU KNOW YOU ARE THE ONLY UGLY ONE RIGHT NOW, RIGHT?!" Rosemary jumped up from her seat trying to make a comeback from my insult to the best of her ability.

"I'd never take that back," I stuck my tongue out at Rosemary and flicked my finger at her eye, "You say I am ugly, but we come from the same people. However, I'm aware of how ugly I am in this judgmental society we live in."

Rosemary turned a violent red, she looked like a blood red rose, holding her eye and she shouted, "I hate you, you stupid menace!" and then just stomped away in a formidable fashion.

I laughed, "Do you know the real definition of it?"

"Yeah, an annoyance," Rosemary stopped in her tracks and was too stuck up for her own good.

I shook my head, "No, it typically has something to do with harming others and threats. You are too off target for me to go into full detail. I'd be a waste on your tiny brain. I'm not a menace, you are."

"Yeah, yeah, you are an idiot 'cause you don't have magic," Maranda rolled her eyes.

"Yeah but bare sakura branches will always grow leaves and cherry blossoms in the spring," I smiled, trying to see if they knew where I was getting at.

"So?" Celeste made a face.

I smirked, "I'm the bare branch with no magic, and once my leaves grow, I get my magic, but some fall in the fall like you going from summer to fall."

"What are you, some poet?" Rosemary snorted. Her friends laughed.

"Yeah, unless you stop treating me like crap, I should throw you in an actual oven and roast you," I lowered my eyebrows, preparing a threat. Threats are common, and not completely illegal unlike in the world you probably live in. I still wasn't fully allowed to make a threat towards a magic blood however, but I think you know me well enough that I'll ignore that biased law, "Alive. And then eat you."

Chapter 15: Joining a Team

Rosemary was in every sport and cheerleading team possible. All of them except for baseball, football, and cricket, which she had no interest playing, no offense, but otherwise she was in all of the sports teams. Every recess, there was a sport that you could play and team leaders choose people to be on their team.

The gym assistants AKA the team leaders choose the people they wanted on their team. I watched as Rosemary, Celeste, and Maranda picked at once by Gym Assistant Coralline. I was very good at sports and was ready to show that to them. I would do any sport to show them my talent. Even my least favorite sport. I never got chosen at all and teams were full so I was forced to leave the field.

There was an archery and sword fighting club that took place at recess but they wouldn't let me participate, so I helped myself to the targets after school. I also helped myself to the ninja course and made it through every stage with ease.

"How are you doing?" Haven asked.

"Good," I smiled, "You?"

"I'm good as well," Haven joined me in archery once I started practicing archery again later that day, "Want to do a small sword fight? I've got the basic rules down."

"Sure," I agreed and listened carefully.

I won 3 times and Haven won 2 and then I won again as a final round. Then we headed back to the building as the sun started to set.

"That was fun!" I exclaimed happily, stretching.

"I agree!" Haven gave me a high-five, "Earlier today, when you roasted Rosemary, that was awesome, she's such a spoiled brat."

"Just you wait, I'll get ya-oww--!" Rosemary came up to us and fell down a hole covered by dried up leaves, "Darn it!"

"You're a spider that falls for her own traps, you have no brain. Also, you know, there is a plant called rosemary and it's edible. People can eat spiders too. Is this the heavens telling me I should eat you?" I retorted, walked around the hole she made for me to fall in, "That trap, I'd give an A for effort, but it's too obvious. It's not gunna work"

Rosemary left saying, "I said I'll get you back!" just like a typical cartoon villain.

The next day, there was a poster saying, 'fighting team! You get to do a fighting tournament with other schools at the end of the year and be school guards! Make new friends! Etc.!' but what I didn't read were tiny words at the bottom.

I was going to join. Lydia, Rose, Haven, and Cai were joining as well. When we walked in the gym, I was wearing the outfit I wore on the first day back here, which was a version of an outfit I wear a lot. I wore it like this when I'm hyped up.

I announced, "My friends and I are here to join the fighting team."

Everyone laughed, even the girls on the gymnastics team and Haven asked, "What?! The poster said we could join, or are you liars?"

"I suppose you didn't read the little note on the poster. Girls can't fight, except for Rosemary, she is absolutely perfect. It's always been this way. Plus, we aren't letting a no-magic join us. You're so stupid! Can't cast a spell," Changle laughed.

My skin was starting to boil with anger, "Alright, Mr. Captain-dude-I-don't-give-a-god-dang-thought-about-the-people-I-make-fun-of! The only pea-brain in the room is you. You think we aren't equal even though we should be. However, not having magic doesn't express who I am on the inside and my skills as a person!"

"Look, Cai can join but not any of you. Come on, you gotta have muscles," Rosemary smiled.

She was the deputy captain of the team.

"Oh?" I rolled my eyes hearing her mocking tone and watched the boys flex at their 'muscles', "Really? What muscles?"

"Frick you, you know what I mean," Rosemary cussed, shooting me a glare.

They tossed stuff at me while I lay on the ground unmoving, reading and eating while blocking the tomatoes being hurled at me. Haven chuckled at their surprised faces.

"My past may be bad, but it has taught me to stay strong and stay on my feet to my last step," I smiled. Attempt 2, be so cheesy, that they can't deal with it anymore and they accept you, "Look, either you accept girls and people with no magic or I will let you guys lose in a battle and die."

"Cheesy much? Girls don't have any ability to fight! Especially people without magic," they shouted. A split second later, a special bell to notify an attack from demons went off.

Changle said, "Rosemary, stay in charge. I am going to keep this little demon out of our way. You guys, with magic, you can go I guess."

Changle held me captive, clearly still upset with me leaving in the first place but I had a secret plan going inside my head.

He held me in a choking position as he said, "How do you like this, devil?"

"I don't mind," I said calmly, "But right now, you seem like a really old disgusting pervert.

Changle made no comment about that.

There was a wall in front of me and I jumped while he had me in the choke hold. I kicked the wall in front of me as hard I could. Changle fell to the ground with a loud thud as I swung around the obstacle course.

"Girls can't jump hurdles!" Changle called, racing after me.

"Hn, keep sayin' that," I leapt over hurdles quickly and jumped around on the parkour. The perk of being skilled with both left and right feet and hands, is that it doesn't matter which leading foot I use when running hurdles.

I grasped onto a bar in a parkour course after the girls left after their gymnastics meet was over. I had to do some monkey bars to get to the door.

I headed for the door as I parkoured and Changle was after me. The door was up high and there were hooks on a bar. Below me, there was a trampoline. I jumped down, landed on the trampoline, and gripped onto the bar above me to get to the door.

I used the bar and hooked the bar higher and higher as I shouted, "You were saying?!"

I raced out the door. There was a demon right in front of Rosemary, ready to kill her. I sliced the head off of the demon mercilessly from behind, glaring at him, and I used a sword I took from Changle without him realizing. To which he then looked left and right for his sword. Rosemary screamed at the head that flew toward her, bonked the wall, and fell into her lap in a bloody mess. Demons are created from people that have ended up losing control of their magic for some reason, one way or the other.

"D-Dawn? What are you doing here?" Rosemary cried in disgust.

Changle finally got to the door, "You come back here!"

"Not a chance!" I stuck out my tongue and shot a demon squarely in the eye with Changle's sword, "If your deputy-captain can't even fight, then this is useless. I'm still waiting for my thank you."

"Thank you," Rosemary grumbled angrily and then muttered a curse word at me.

"It's over," Every pointed their spears at me after the battle was over as Rosemary held up a gun and I leaned on a wall, tossing a ball up and down. I had brought the ball with me from the gym.

"What now?" I grumbled. *Same crap every day, I tell you.*

"You will die, of course. It's truly something that we didn't bring police to hold you back and put you in jail for breaking so many laws already," Rosemary declared, "And you know girls can't fight here."

"You are a girl too, you know," I glared.

"Well, I'm the exception. I the virtuoso of the school and I also have magic," Rosemary snapped.

"No, you can try to kill her but she won't die forever. I can revive certain people," Cai snapped back at Rosemary.

"Too late," Rosemary shot her sword and smiled.

I caught the sword in my hand swiftly, blade in my hand. My hand was bleeding in my black fingerless glove, but it wasn't that big of a deal. I then fired it back at Rosemary as she screamed and ducked. I had only thrown it. Rosemary was so weak and pathetic. She's so hypocritical and she says she's the best. I think I just beat her in that one. Attempt 3? Prove them terribly wrong.

Changle rolled his eyes in annoyance, "Fine, you win, you can fight."

"Yes!!!" I smirked and leapt right over the blades, on top of Rosemary's head, and left the scene with an angry Rosemary sitting on the ground, in pain, clutching her head.

At night, after I explained everything that happened to the Forest family. I exclaimed with excitement, "I can't believe it, I am allowed on the team! I'm so excited! Don't let other people know I said that though, lol."

Chapter 16: A Christmas Surprise

I yawned, waking up and I walked over to my calendar to mark it and when I did, realization hit me, "Merry Christmas everyone!"

They smiled and shouted in happiness, "You too and happy 13th birthday!"

"Thank you!" I beamed. It was hard to believe I was already thirteen!

I sat waiting for everyone to sit down at the Christmas tree in our common room chamber, which was filled with presents under the tree. Lights and garlands decorated the originally boring artificial tree.

We went out for bubble tea and the school had a campfires and s'mores for the Christmas celebration. The school also had cookies and hot chocolate and brownies for everyone.

I gave Cai some medical tools for Christmas, I gave Haven a Moon and Cloud plushie, Lydia received a coral reef pendant from me, and I got Rose a rosebush in a pot. We laughed endlessly at funny times and funny things Rosemary always deserved and at night, we even had a pillow fight

Everyone was in such a good mood at night, everyone didn't want to go to sleep but it was good that sleepiness later took over each other us by 10:57.

As weeks passed by, I was in many school teams and people talked about me in the hallways. Good things about me anyhow. It was good for a change. I was a nice upbeat person, I think I am at least, and brought a smile to everyone. Well... almost everyone.

I had made it as one of the top 10 students at the school. Actually, if you were wondering. I was 2nd best but Rosemary was keeping her role as first place student.

"We are going to see who is in first place in the end of the year. Bet it's me, you in?" Rosemary asked.

"Yeah, but you mean, you know I **am** going to win," I agreed.

"You know, the first place at the end of the year is judged based on the speech you give in the last week of school. Its 1st place student vs 2nd place student," Rosemary was smug about her long lasting first place, "Oh, and when you are in first place in the end of the year, you get a wish."

"I know what I am gonna wish for," *equal rights for everyone.* I said and then thought.

"If I win you die, if you win, I die," Rosemary was way too smug and sure of herself and casted a spell while speaking.

"Alright. But don't you have a terminal illness?" I shrugged, "Cai can revive me and that isn't part of the bet that he can't revive me so yeah. I'm out of here."

Rosemary rolled her eyes, "you doubt me. If I win, I'm using my wish to not be terminally ill."

There was no one to revive Rosemary yet so if she died, she died. I didn't care if she died. She never was really part of my life. She just a page torn from my story, my life. I would no longer be in her evil shadow. I'm my own person, not someone who doesn't care about me, chose to define me as.

The next morning, I saw my classmate, Sanita crying and I asked her, "What's wrong?"

"My cat died, my brother just told me and he never lies so I know it's true," Sanita sniffled.

"Hey, it's okay, can't you revive him or something? I mean I heard that you could revived people and animals you loved," I sat next to her.

A smile spread across her face, "Your right! Thank you, Dawn! I gonna revive Snowy when I get home."

When she got back, a bigger smile was on her face and I asked, "Well?"

Sanita began, "My brother lied to get me back home, to get me a new cat! Plus, Snowy didn't even die! But I'm still mad at him about it."

I was happy for her and jokingly said with a smile, "Nice! That's so cool! Don't kill your brother for it!"

"Thanks for being a wonderful person," Sanita chuckled at my joke and left and I smiled back.

We hugged each other and exchanged compliments and went back to our dorms.

"Hey, you do have a power," Sarah smiled and mumbled to herself, "Of happiness and laugher."

"What?" I asked.

"Oh, nothing," Sarah replied, "I was talking to myself."

"Oh, okay," I went to bed, "Good night."

"You too," Sarah floated away

I fell asleep quickly in the soft bed and so was my family. I couldn't wait to March 31st to come. I was bursting with anticipation.

Chapter 17: Another Family Photo

When March 31st finally rolled around, I shouted in front of my family's dorm doors with delight, "Family Picture Day!"

"Yesss!" Haven ran out of her room, already dressed.

"Mreow?" Lily mewed tilting her head as she sat on my head. Lily was brought over from the non-magic island.

Once we all got ready, we went to take our photos. We brought out pets along, Lily and Flame on my shoulders and Aurora on my head holding a ball of yarn in her hands.

"The brown-and-black-haired girl, stand in the middle," the photographer pointed at me, "Blue girl and green girl, and kneel down next to her, on each side. Purple and brown guys, sit next to blue and green girls. Pets in front."

After that, we did a pyramid like shape, I was on top. Haven and Hiro were beneath me holding me up. Under Haven, there was a few chairs and Rose since there were only 5 of us to make the human pyramid.

The little pets played around under the chairs Winter and Cory sat next to Rose. Grey and Alex sat next to Lydia, who was on the side of a pyramid.

Chapter 18: Choosing Who

Changle soon opened up to me since I gave the Magic Kingdom another chance, I guess. He was less mad with me, at the very least. Changle announced things about the upcoming tournament.

Changle said, "I choose all 50 of us, since some of us left in the middle of the year. For the last tournament, the judge chooses one position to switch sides. If it isn't captain or deputy captain, then the judge would choose 2 people from each side to switch sides. And they aren't allowed to help the team they come from."

I listened carefully and I got ready for the first challenge. The first challenge was where you choose a weapon or no weapon at all, to fight against people in a tournament. The goal was to get 1st place and you couldn't switch weapons between battles either.

I chose to not have a weapon and everyone thought I was crazy but I was sure about my choice. Reloading an arrow and getting distance would be hard and even worse if they picked a bow and arrow as well. The 1st event took place on May 26, the 2nd was on June 2nd, and the last was on June 9th.

Changle finished up, "I will tell you more about the second event next week, 2 nights before the event, and the last event 3 nights before the event so we can settle positions and explain rules."

"Alright!" I left after Changle declared that the meeting was terminated.

I prepared and packed my things to go to Paris, France the next morning. The second place was at Tianjing, China. The last event was at our school. It was May 24th today.

I finished packing and rode a night bus to the airport. I went on the plane with my things. Since it was 1:45 AM, I was practically yawning up a storm. My legs and lower back were in absolute pain.

"I am gonna take a nap on the plane," I continued to yawn.

"Okay," Cai smiled, "I will too."

"I am not tired," Haven sat, wide awake, "Probably because I am dark type and they can stay awake for a long time without getting tired."

We went to the hotel and flopped into bed. The soft mattress, pillow, soft yet comfy blanket was so comforting. There's not really much to describe.

The next day, the day of the fighting tournament, I was up first VS 曹风(Cao-Feng), the captain of the Chinese team. I won fair and square quickly enough. Haven was against Kwame form Africa and Lydia was up against Juliana from Brazil. Cai was against Victor N. and Changle was pleased to see Cai beat him.

Rose was against Bom from Korea. Changle was against Aito from Japan. I then went against some other people I couldn't quite get the name of. Only Cai, Changle, Rosemary and I were close to being in the semi-finals.

"Now moving on to semi-finals... are Changle and Dawn from America, Victor S. from France, and Juliana from Brazil!" Tha announcer called out in English and then in France.

"Woo!" Each team hooted for their players that were in the semi-finals.

I won the semi-finals match and the Announcer announced, "In the finals are the two competitors... Juliana Brathate of Brazil and Dawn Heathens of America!"

I won the match! I was so excited I thought it had to be a lie. To be honest, Juliana was tough. Changle always tells me I'm one tough opponent to beat. Especially so, since I didn't have magic. We were ranked and got medals. I earned a trophy for America, Washington, and my school. Changle got 4th and didn't win anything except a participation medal like everyone else who didn't get 1st, 2nd, or 3rd place.

Changle wasn't mad since we still won the 1st tournament in the end.

On May 31st, Changle checked his clipboard, "Okay, so, next week, the game is in China, the tournament is... drumroll... an archery tournament, so let's get practicing and afterward, go pack and get to the bus to get to the plane."

"Alright!" I was already at the archery field before others.

"Just saying, later in the archery course, there will be moving targets and you moving and both. Who gets the best score wins," Changle said, shooting and arrow while running across the field.

"Dude!" I shouted, ducking, "Aim! You almost hit me!"

"Sorry, I have never done archery before. I have done fencing and sword-fighting. I need help with archery," Changle scratched his head in an apology.

"You really do. No one should be that bad first try," I sat on my new horse, Coconut, "How can you shoot forward and end up the arrow moving backwards?"

Coconut was completely white with some brown spots. She was quick and speedy. Her beady black eyes looked promising. My hair was tied back in two pigtails. I was in my signature outfit, which isn't surprising at all.

I prepared to shoot an arrow at a target and it landed squarely in the middle. Then I got off Coconut, and Changle brought the auto-moving arrow target out and stood aside. I also shot it squarely in the center and I then went back on Coconut and shot from there and 2 arrows were close to the center but it didn't hit bull's eye.

I lunched another arrow and watched it fly and hit the center. Quite a few other people did it as well. Some, first timers even, showing Changle up. Cai, Haven, Lydia, and Rose of course got the same result as I did.

"Woah!" Everyone was amazed, "I think we are going to win this! Yeah!!!"

"I've had tons of practice. There's archery club back at the island," I replied calmly, "And we have gifted people here. And, if you've forgotten, there's an archery club here too."

"And whichever team from any country wins the most rounds, wins. Other countries have other events but we are going to be against China for this. We win, we will go against Brazil next time. If we lose, China will go against Brazil and we will fight Japan for second place I think." Changle tried to sort things out.

"Get everything straight before you say it, you are making me confused, kind-of I guess," I told Changle who was still messing things up and then saying what he said earlier was correct, "Third place, not second. Japan would be second."

"Okay, I'll stop," Changle sighed.

I was on the plane, waiting to land when Changle started dancing like crazy in his seat. People starred at him like he was crazy, not that he wasn't. Turns out he was just dancing to music through his headphones.

I sat still, embarrassed by Changle dancing in his seat next to me. Changle danced his way out of the airport while people gave him weird looks. I knew the song he was listening to. I liked it too, but he's a bit open and embarrassing about it. It had become morning by the time we landed.

"I don't know him," I said in Chinese to everyone when they looked at me. How did I not manage to know Changle's weird side? Good lord, "我不知道这个人。(I don't know this person)"

Changle was dancing while walking and I pulled his headphones off and jerked him back on the sidewalk before he could be crushed by a bus.

"What was that for?!" Changle reached for his headphones.

I held it high up, not letting him reach it, "You were dancing and weren't paying attention to your surroundings. You almost got killed by a bus. Be happy I frickin' saved you."

"Until we get to the hotel, Dawn is going keep the headphones," Haven smirked, clearly knowing what I was thinking.

"But she is listening to music too!" Changle complained.

"But she's paying attention to her surrounding unlike you," Lydia commented.

"Fine whatever," Changle rolled his eyes.

"Halt!" I said, "Cars."

"See?" Rose pointed out.

"Okay, okay, you guys win," Changle held his hands up.

"On the bright side," Cai said aloud, "If Dawn didn't stop you, we would have one less person to shoot our asses like practice earlier."

Cai was talking about Rosemary being shot on her butt and having to stay at school and rest after being healed. Rosemary would be able to attend to last event but not today's because of Changle's horrible aiming skills.

"I said I don't use bows and arrows," Changle shrugged.

"But then you can't be that bad," I pointed out to Changle.

"Whatever, look, no one in my family knows how to use bows and arrows," Changle insisted that he was innocent.

On the day of the tournament, I got bull's eye perfectly repeatedly for still shots, 1-thing-moving shots, and for the-double-moving shots. Then again, so many of our teammates did, so my score was nothing special.

"The winner is... Team Magic Academy, Magic Island, Washington, America!" the announcer announced in both Chinese and English fluently.

I understood the Chinese since I studied multiple languages back at the Non-Magic Island. We still lived in the alternate dimension/universe where magic and magical creatures weren't possible in the other dimension.

Some priests travel to the other dimension/universe and try to understand and learn more about their universe/dimension.

Practice with my weapons really helped me here.

"Good job! You got most of our points," Changle gave me, a high-five.

I joked, "I noticed you almost shot an opponent's face this time and got disqualified. Also, Haven actually got most of the points."

"Whatever!" Changle rolled his eyes playfully. *Should I be suspicious with his man? Is he hitting on me? Nah, its fine.*

Later that week, Changle announced, "Here are some rules for the game which is the tournament that is against Brazil. You know, that one?"

"Uh-huh," Everyone nodded.

Changle continued, "The game is kind of like Capture the Flag but Capture the trophy, I guess. We are white team which means we get more rules. Each team has 30 warriors, 10 castle guards, and 10 trophy protectors. No magic except for transformations which means no flying."

"What are the rules?" I asked. This June, I was an angel, instead of a demon. However, Valor and Bri remained demons.

"The judges will say," Changle skipped the rules, "But here are some rules for everyone. Only the warriors can go and try to get the trophy unless a trophy protector gets a Sword of Faith for us and Sword of Death for the other team. The warriors will be all over the place, guards will be on the outside, and protectors will be on the inside, protecting the trophy and the 3 entrances. 3 protectors will be at each entrance, and 1 protector will guard the trophy right next to it."

"And Protectors can switch their 'Protector' positions but a guard can't become a warrior or vice versa and a warrior can't become a protector or vice versa. I think you get the idea. You can't change positions," Rosemary added

"Correct," Changle smiled, "And if you are 'killed' by someone, you're out. If you're on the black team, all you have to do is grab the trophy but since we are white team, the unlucky team, we have to bring it back safely, and place it on top of our own. Judges will be everywhere to see if you are playing it the way it should. This was not created to be a racist game. It was a way to see how people confronted odds being stacked aganst them."

"If it's a miner mistake you make, the other team gets to still go while our team is frozen for 15 seconds. If it is medium, then you are 'dead and if it is a big, unacceptable mistake, you are 'dead' and we are frozen for a minute," Rosemary looked serious but she wasn't really talking to me even though I listened the whole time.

The rules of that game. The white side, is just like me, and the black side (not to be racist, I promise. I didn't create this. I cross my heart and hope to die) was society.

With some quick healing magic, Rosemary was up and running.

Chapter 21: The Tournament Part 3

I was ready to go, my hair was in two low pigtails, and I was in my signature outfit. It was loose yet fitting, and I was wearing good athletic shoes. I was ready, in my protector position, keeping the trophy safe. The sword I was to use, was next to me, at the ready.

"The deputy captains shall switch places which means Rosemary Super of America and Vonia Dontre of Brazil will exchange places.

After the judge blew his whistle, it was in complete chaos, one entrance's door busted opened and I slashed him and became "dead," but got revived by the judge. Haven, Rose, and Lydia quickly replaced the door and screwed it in nice and tight.

"Remember the only way you can join in the battle field is when you have to sword of faith," a judge reminded me.

"I know," I rolled my eyes while searching for it.

Just as I found it, a man busted a different door and I 'killed' him. I went back to the sword but the sword had moved so I tried to find it again. Another person busted in and I 'murdered' him back then, the sword was gone again. I found it again, and it teleported away faster than I could blink and took it the split second I found it again. I came out of the castle with the gold and white sword bejeweled with colorful gems. For the poor created rules, we sure get a good looking sword.

It was 1 hour into the game and it ended in 15 minutes. There had been so many break-in's from our area that we were low on replacement doors.

I hit the guards on the "black" team, and dodging side to side, dodging blows, throwing stars, and kunai knifes. I kicked open the door, ducked the swords, and made it to the trophy room with a bit of luck and help on my side.

The question was, could I make it back without 'dying'? Getting out was harder since, people surrounded me from all sides and they were inching closer to me. I ran about and ducked, perfectly slipping through the circle of Protectors. Our warriors distracted several of the other team's warriors. I only had to outrace Rosemary. Which, too be frank, wasn't too hard.

I only had 1 minute to get back and place the trophy on my own team's trophy. I had to outrun the other team. If no one got a trophy, black would automatically win.

I ran so fast, I think I got back to the castle in 45 seconds and I had to place the trophy down in 15 seconds. I was literally too out of breath to walk a few more steps and place it down. I tossed it over to Lydia, over the other team's waving hands when I reached the door. Just as the buzzer rang, she placed it down just in time.

"And... White team wins!" the judge announced.

"Yes!", "Yass!", "OMG!", and, "We won!" from my teammates.

The judge smiled, "The International Warrior Cup goes to America and is the very third white team to win!!!"

"Really?" I was shocked, "Okay, but that is really wrong. Ya'll need to change things."

"Yeah! We won! We won! We won!" Changle chanted.

Meanwhile, I was collapsing to the floor, completely out of breath.

Chapter 22: My Power

Do you think I'll ever get magic, Sarah?" I asked doubtfully.

"I like to think of everyone having their own unique power, even if it isn't actual magic," Sarah replied, "I like to think of you, having the power to bring smiles and laughter to people's faces."

"You think so?" I asked.

"Yep, you also make me smile and laugh, you bake cookies for me when Mom and Dad are out of town or when I am upset. You make others smile too. I also like to think you have the mini of super-intelligence since you are really smart but you also have a unique one-of-a-kind fighting ability," Sarah reasoned.

"And you have the power to make imaginary powers for people who don't have magic," I joked, "I should get ready for my speech in a few days. I haven't thought of what to say."

I thought hard for hours and I finally came up with the perfect idea for my speech and my topic, remembering my talk with Sarah. I got started right away and practiced and practiced day and night non-stop until I memorized it completely. A few times, Sarah pretended to be my audience which was really nice of her to do.

Rosemary was up first, "What's up Magicals! I think that we should build a better community where it's a better world where only Magicals live. Just like we always have. Nothing has to change and we can keep striving for the top. I am here to help build a better community as always and like every year. We are here to become more powerful, Magicals! So, then we can stand up stronger and prouder. I will lead us through it if I become 1st place. Just think about it. What if we lived without bad and without magicless people."

I raised my hand, "But what would the world be without bad, huh? If something bad happened, no one would be brave enough to face it, the world wouldn't be balanced the way it should. If something bad did occur they wouldn't dare even try to defend, and we would be WEAK without bad. If bad wasn't here to make us braver and stronger, where would we be? And, what defines the bad? What is the border between the two? Something good in one's eyes, may be bad in another pair of ideas."

Rosemary glared and continued, "Watch your mouth. You shouldn't speak so carefree towards someone of high level status. Us magic people are higher than those without for our gift of magic. It's our magic that defines us. We were the normal ones around. There's more of us due to natural selection, after all, If you want another amazing year, choose me!"

Rosemary left the stage with people throwing flowers, and others cheering for her. I felt a bit discouraged but it was too late to turn back. Her speech couldn't have been that good. And I'd done too much work to ditch it last minute. Sometimes and life, people pick others because they are alike. Or because it's always been that way, and people don't like change.

I walked up to the stage, eyeballs staring at me like I'm some sort of outlier in a museum, "To be honest, everyone is equal, girl or man, magic or no magic, light skin or dark, we should all be treated equally. A friend of mine helped me realize that everyone's special power is in our heart even if we don't actually have magic, cheesy as it is. We have our own inner abilities like Sanita's inner power of kindness, love, friendship, truth, generosity, empathy, and helping others."

A girl said, "Can I have another example?"

"Sure," I replied, "Another example is Changle's never-ending ability to stand back up and try again no matter the cost and helping others before himself even if it means risking his own life to save their lives. We all have inner powers so it doesn't matter if I don't have magic. My friend, Sarah says, my inner power is bring smiles and laughter to people and intelligence."

"Gotta finish up soon," Changle's dad looked at his watch.

I hurried up, trying not to pass the time limit and I ended up silently laughing at the last sentence, "I never had magic but it has never let me down or knocked me to the ground to the point I can't get back up. Plus, remember, the world must be balanced like Yin and Yang, good has some bad, and bad has some good. Thank you for listening and I respect your decision if you choose your long-lasted leader, Rosemary. Sometimes people choose how things have always gone, I will not force you to choose me. Thank you for listening to be blabber about nothing."

Rosemary and I weren't allowed to vote so we sat on the side. We were also not allowed to look at the ballets. Later, Changle's mom looked at all the ballets and there were only 3982 for Rosemary. The others all voted for me but I didn't know just yet, since only Changle's parents knew.

The speaker announced, "And the 1st place, is... Dawn Heathens! The ballets scored 4674 - 3982, the 3982, being Rosemary's votes!"

"What?!?!?!" Rosemary raged but according to the bet, she died a few hours later. Nothing surprising there.

I couldn't believe it, so many people voted for me! I was so excited. Everyone chattered about the new leader of the year. I didn't even care or grieve over her death. She was part of my real family, but she isn't part of my family anymore. I had a new family that loves each other. She never cared about me, after all, she was the one who said my life was none of her business, like I could jump off the Golden Gate Bridge and she wouldn't care.

Changle's mom continued, "And what will your wish be? Oh wait, we need to get to the traditional wishing ground. My bad."

We all gathered at the sacred garden and I said, "I wish for, equal rights, no matter their gender, skin, or magic ability."

Chapter 24: My Wish

My wish symbolized equal rights for everyone, they made a bridge to get to each island quickly and efficiently. The people on the non-magic island filled with glee as they explored the magic island.

A warm sensation came over me as I smiled and noticed this fairy was tapping her wand on my head.

I screamed, "Ahhh! Who's there?!"

"Sorry," the fairy said with a wink, "The name's Sarah."

The fairy looked oddly familiar but I knew it couldn't be Sarah from the forest family.

The fairy said, "I am the fairy of powers. Even though, you have don't have magic blood to even allow you to get magic but everyone has their own power inside them.

"I've heard that before," I sighed, still upset that I couldn't have magic, but it didn't me too much.

"Bummer," Cai frowned.

Even though I didn't have magic, I gave my new— well, not so new family, a hug.

Haven raised her eyebrows up and down when I gave Cai a hug, "Ship! Ship! Ship! I ship Cai and Dawn! Their ship name is Cawn!"

"Cawn! Cawn! Cawn!" Haven chanted as people followed.

"My real name is Caimalynn but uh—okay," Cai shrugged.

"Come back here!" I shouted playfully, chasing after Haven.

We started chasing each other playfully as the garden filled with laughter and chants of Cawn. Cai and I ran away from the laughing mob, in different directions.

I don't think Haven's gunna tease me about it anytime soon without a full suit of armor. As for everyone else, I spared them this time.

Author's note

I think that even if our world has no magic, we can always bring smiles, friendship, kindness, and balance into the world like fighting for equal rights. Dawn, she has never had magic but she was still able to bring smiles and laughter to others as her inner power. Everyone has an inner power.

Also, this is very important. Kids, you shouldn't run away from home if you feel unneeded in your family. You are very much needed in your family. Also, you probably won't survive very long. My point is, this is a fictional book, not real life. Don't try to do this.

Credit to a friend of mine, where I took their term of "Suck it up, buttercup." I did not come up with it, sadly.

I'd also like to say thank you to all those people who helped review and read my book in its writing and editing stages, including some friends of mine (I'm not listing names, because that's private information).

Thank you for reading Cursed Into the Shadows! It was so fun to write, cringy and messy or not.

About the author

I love to write(no duh, I wrote this whole book ^^ haha) and I love cats, art, crafting things, and I love to Ice skate, play basketball, and do karate. I love making puns, I'm good at math, and love hanging out with friends.

I have written a private books series that isn't and won't be published. It isn't exactly private since I have shared it to some people.

Even though I love cats, I don't own any of my own. I spend a lot of my time writing and doing homework for school and from my parents. I really enjoy watching anime and reading manga. My favorite being Pokémon, and second favorite being Naruto, and another favorite being A Silent Voice. I also love Aphmau's MyStreet series.

I'll be working on another book in the meantime, called Sisters of Discs.

www.ingramcontent.com/pod-product-compliance
Lightning Source LLC
Chambersburg PA
CBHW051924220626
47052CB00003B/572